The Nightingale

HANS CHRISTIAN ANDERSEN

The Nightingale

ILLUSTRATED BY IGOR OLEYNIKOV

PURPLE BEAR BOOKS

NEW YORK

In China, you know, the emperor is Chinese, and all his people are Chinese, too. This story happened a great many years ago, so it is well to hear it now before it is forgotten.

The emperor's palace was the most beautiful in the world. It was built entirely of porcelain that was very costly and so delicate that anyone who touched it had to be very careful not to break it. In the garden there were the most beautiful flowers, with pretty silver bells tied to them that tinkled, so that everyone who passed could not help noticing them. Indeed, everything in the emperor's garden was remarkable, and it extended so far that the gardener himself did not know where it ended. Those who traveled beyond its limits knew that there was a great forest with lofty trees sloping down to the deep blue sea, where great ships sailed under the shadow of its branches. In one of these trees lived a nightingale, who sang so beautifully that even the poor fishermen, who were very busy, would stop and listen. Sometimes, when they went at night to spread their nets, they would hear her sing and would say, "Oh, isn't that beautiful!" But when they returned to their fishing, they forgot the bird until the next night. Then they would hear her again, and exclaim, "Oh, how beautiful is the nightingale's song!"

Travelers from every country in the world came to the emperor's city, which they admired very much, as well as the palace and gardens. But when they heard the nightingale, they all declared it to be the best thing of all. And the travelers, on their return home, related what they had seen, and learned men wrote books, containing descriptions of the town, the palace, and the gardens. They did not forget the nightingale, which was really the greatest wonder of all. Poets composed beautiful verses about the nightingale, who lived in the forest near the deep sea. The books traveled all over the world, and some of them came into the hands of the emperor.

The emperor sat on his golden throne reading them, and, as he read, he nodded his approval, for it pleased him to find such a beautiful description of his city, his palace, and his gardens. But when he came to the words, "The nightingale is the most beautiful of all," he exclaimed, "What is this? I know nothing of any nightingale. Is there such a bird in my empire—in my own garden? I have never heard of it. It appears something may indeed be learned from books."

Then he called one of his lords-in-waiting, who was so high-bred that when anyone of an inferior rank spoke to him or asked him a question, he would answer, "Pfoo," which means nothing.

"There is a very wonderful bird mentioned here, called a nightingale," said the emperor. "They say it is the best thing in my kingdom. Why haven't I been told of it?"

"I have never heard of it," replied the lord-in-waiting. "She has not been presented at court."

"It is my pleasure that she come and sing for me this evening," said the emperor. "The whole world knows what I possess better than I do myself."

"I have never heard of her," said the lord-in-waiting. "But I will try to find her."

But where was the nightingale to be found? The lord-in-waiting went up stairs and down, through halls and passages; yet no one he met had heard of the bird. So he returned to the emperor and said that it must be a fable, invented by those who had written the books. "Your Imperial Majesty," he said, "you cannot believe everything contained in books. Sometimes they are only fiction, or what is called the black art."

"But the book in which I have read this account," said the emperor, "was sent to me by the great and mighty emperor of Japan, and therefore it must be true. I will hear the nightingale this evening, and if she does not come, the whole court shall be beaten after supper is ended."

"Tsing-pe!" cried the lord-in-waiting, and again he ran up and down stairs, through all the halls and corridors, in and out of the palace, and half the court ran with him, for they did not like the idea of being beaten. They asked all they met about this wonderful nightingale known to all the world except the court.

At last they met a poor little girl, who said, "Oh, yes, I know the nightingale quite well and indeed she can sing. Every evening I have permission to take the scraps from the table home to my poor, sick mother who lives by the shore. As I come back I am so tired that I sit and rest in the woods and listen to the nightingale's song. Then the tears come into my eyes, and it is just as if my mother were kissing me."

"Little maiden," said the lord-in-waiting, "I will get you a steady job in the palace kitchen and you shall have permission to see the emperor dine, if you will lead us to the nightingale, for she is invited to sing at the palace this evening."

So she went into the woods where the nightingale sang, and half the court followed her.

As they went along, a cow began lowing.

"Oh," said a young courtier, "now we have found her! What wonderful power for such a small creature. I have certainly heard it before."

"No, that is only a cow lowing," said the little girl. "We still have a long way to go."

Then some frogs began to croak in the marsh.

"Beautiful," said the young courtier again. "Now I hear it, tinkling like little church bells."

"No, those are frogs," said the little maiden. "But I think we shall soon hear her." And presently the nightingale began to sing.

"Hark, hark! There she is," said the girl, pointing to a little gray bird who was perched on a bough.

"Is it possible?" said the lord-in-waiting. "I never imagined it would be such a plain little thing as that. All her color must have drained away at the sight of so many people here."

"Little nightingale," cried the girl, "our most gracious emperor wishes you to sing before him."

"With the greatest pleasure," said the nightingale, and began to sing most delightfully.

"It sounds like tiny glass bells," said the lord-in-waiting. "And see how her little throat works. It is surprising that we have never heard this before. She will be a great success at court."

"Shall I sing once more before the emperor?" asked the nightingale, who thought he was present.

"My excellent little nightingale," said the lord-in-waiting, "I have the great pleasure of inviting you to the palace this evening, where you will gain imperial favor by your charming song."

"My song sounds best in the green woods," said the bird, but still she came willingly when she heard the emperor's wish.

The palace was elegantly decorated for the occasion. The walls and floors of porcelain glittered in the light of a thousand lamps. Beautiful flowers, tied with little bells, stood in the corridors. In the center of the great hall, a golden perch had been set for the nightingale. The little girl, now officially called kitchen maid, had received permission to stand by the door. The whole court was present, all dressed in their best, and every eye was turned to the little gray bird. The emperor nodded to her to begin. The nightingale sang so sweetly that the tears rose in the emperor's eyes and rolled down his cheeks. Then the nightingale sang even more beautifully, and her song went right to his heart.

The emperor was so delighted that he declared the nightingale should have his gold slipper to wear around her neck, but she declined the honor with thanks saying, "I have seen tears in the emperor's eyes. That is my richest reward. An emperor's tears have wonderful power and are quite enough honor for me." Then she sang again more enchantingly than ever.

"That singing is a lovely gift," said the ladies of the court to one another. Then they poured water into their mouths, trying to trill like the nightingale. The footmen and chambermaids also expressed their satisfaction, which is saying a great deal, for they are very difficult to please. In fact the nightingale's visit was most successful. She was now to remain at court, to have her own cage, with liberty to go out twice a day, and once during the night. Twelve servants were to go with her, each holding a silken string fastened to her leg. There was certainly not much pleasure flying like that!

The whole city was talking about the wonderful bird, and when two people met, one said "night," and the other said "gale," and they understood what was meant, for nothing else was talked of. Eleven peddlers' children were named after her, but none of them could sing a note.

One day the emperor received a large parcel with "nightingale" written on it.

"This must be a new book about our celebrated bird," said the emperor.

But instead of a book, it was a work of art, a mechanical toy in a box, an artificial nightingale made to look like a living one, but covered all over with gold and precious jewels. When the artificial bird was wound up, it sang like the real one and moved its tail up and down, shining silver and gold. Around its neck hung a ribbon, on which was written "The Emperor of Japan's nightingale is a poor thing compared with that of the Emperor of China."

"How beautiful!" exclaimed all who saw it, and the man who had delivered the artificial bird received the title of "Imperial Nightingale-Bringer."

"Now they must sing together," said the court, "and what a duet it will be!" But it did not sound quite right, for the real nightingale sang in its own natural way, while the artificial bird sang only waltzes.

"That is not the new bird's fault," said the music master. "It keeps perfect time and sings exactly to my taste." So then it had to sing alone, and was as successful as the real bird. Besides, it was so much prettier to look at, for it sparkled like jewelry. It sang the same tunes thirty-three times without growing tired. The people would gladly have heard it again, but the emperor said the living nightingale ought to sing something. But where was she? No one had noticed when she flew out the open window, back to her own green woods.

"What strange conduct," said the emperor, when her flight had been discovered, and all the courtiers blamed her and said she was a very ungrateful creature.

"But we have the best bird after all," said one, and then they had the bird sing again. Although it was the thirty-fourth time they had listened to the same piece, they still hadn't learned it, for it was rather difficult. The music master praised the bird and even asserted that it was better than the real nightingale, not only in its dress of splendid gold, but also in its musical power. "For you see," he told the court, "with a real nightingale we can never tell what is going to be sung, but with this bird everything is settled. It can be opened and explained, so that people may understand how the song is formed and why one note follows another."

"That is exactly what we think," they all replied, and then the music master received permission to exhibit the bird to the people on the following Sunday, and the emperor commanded that they should be present to hear it sing. When they heard it they were intoxicated, as if from drinking tea, which is a Chinese custom. They all said, "Oh!" and pointed their fingers in the air and nodded. But a poor fisherman, who had heard the real nightingale, said, "It sounds pretty enough, and almost like the real bird, but there seems to be something missing. I don't know what."

After this, the real nightingale was banished from the empire, and the artificial bird placed on a silk cushion close to the emperor's bed. The presents of gold and precious stones it had been given were placed around the bird and it was given the title "Imperial Bedside Singer" and elevated to the rank of number one on the left, for the emperor considered the left side, on which the heart lies, as the most noble, and the heart of an emperor is in the same place as that of other people.

The music master wrote a work in twenty-five volumes about the artificial bird. It was very learned and very long and full of the most difficult Chinese words. All the people said they had read it and understood it, for fear of being thought stupid and being beaten.

So a year passed, and the emperor, the court, and all the other Chinese knew every little turn in the artificial bird's song by heart and it pleased them all the more for they could sing with the bird, which they often did. The boys in the street sang, "Zi-zi-zi, cluck, cluck, cluck," and the emperor himself could sing it, too. It was really most amusing.

One evening, when the artificial bird was singing its best and the emperor lay in bed listening to it, something inside the bird went *whizz*. Then a spring cracked. *Whir-r-r-r* went all the wheels, and then the music stopped. The emperor immediately sprang out of bed and called for his physician, but what could he do?

Then they sent for a watchmaker and, after a great deal of talking and examination, he put the bird into something like order, but he said that it must be used very carefully, as the cylinders were worn and it would be impossible to put in new ones without spoiling the music. Now there was great sorrow as the bird could only be played once a year and even that was dangerous for the works inside it. The music master made a little speech, full of difficult words, and declared that the bird was as good as ever, and of course no one contradicted him.

Five years passed, and then a real sorrow came upon the land. The Chinese really were fond of their emperor, and he now lay so ill that he was not expected to live. Already a new emperor had been chosen and the people who stood in the street asked the lord-in-waiting how the old emperor was, but he only said, "Pfoo!" and shook his head.

Cold and pale lay the emperor in his royal bed. The whole court thought he was dead and ran off to pay homage to the new emperor. Cloth had been laid in the halls so that no footsteps would be heard, and all was silent and still. But the emperor was not yet dead, although he lay white and stiff on his bed. The poor emperor opened his eyes and saw Death sitting there wearing the emperor's golden crown and holding his sword of state and royal banner. All around the bed were strange heads. These were the emperor's good and bad deeds, which stared at him, saying, "Do you remember this?" "Do you recollect that?" They reminded the emperor of so many things that sweat stood out on his brow.

"Music! Music!" cried the emperor. "Make music so that I will not hear what they say. You, little precious golden bird, sing, pray sing! I have given you gold and costly presents. I have even hung my golden slipper around your neck. Sing! Sing!" But the bird remained silent. There was no one to wind it up, and therefore it could not sing a note.

Death continued to stare at the emperor with his cold, hollow eyes, and the room was fearfully still.

Suddenly there came through the open window the sound of sweet music, and in flew the living nightingale. She had come to sing of hope and trust. As she sang, the shadows grew paler and the emperor grew stronger and rose from his bed. Even Death listened and said, "Go on, little nightingale."

"Then will you give back the emperor's sword, banner, and crown?" asked the bird.

So Death gave up these treasures for a song. The nightingale sang of the Devil's garden in the quiet churchyard, and the Devil longed to go there. He swirled into a huge wind that swept up all the strange faces and carried them out the window behind him.

"Thanks, thanks, you heavenly little bird," said the emperor. "I know you well. I banished you from my kingdom once, and yet you have charmed away the evil faces from my bed and banished Death from my heart with your sweet song. How can I reward you?"

"You have already rewarded me," said the nightingale. "I shall never forget that I drew tears from your eyes the first time I sang to you. These are the jewels that rejoice a singer's heart. But now sleep and grow strong and well. I will sing to you again."

As she sang, the emperor fell into a sweet sleep, and how gentle and refreshing that slumber was! When he awoke, strengthened and restored, the sun shone brightly through the window and not one of his servants had returned— they all believed he was dead. Only the nightingale still sat beside him and sang.

"You must always remain with me," said the emperor. "You shall sing only when it pleases you and I will break the artificial bird into a thousand pieces."

"No, do not do that," replied the nightingale. "The bird did its best as long as it could. Keep it here. I cannot live or nest in the palace, but let me come when I like. I will sit on a bough outside your window in the evening and sing to you to gladden your heart and fill it with joy. I will sing to you of those who are happy and those who suffer, of the good and the evil around you. A little singing bird flies far and wide, from your court to the poor fisherman and the peasant's hut. I love your heart better than your crown, and yet something holy lingers around it, too. I will come. I will sing to you, but you must promise me one thing."

"Anything," said the emperor, who had dressed himself in his imperial robes and stood holding his heavy golden sword and royal banner.

"I only ask one thing," she replied. "Let no one know that you have a little bird who tells you everything. It will be best to conceal it." So saying, the nightingale flew away.

The servants, led by the little kitchen maid, now came to look at the dead emperor. To their astonishment, there he stood and said, "Good morning."

Adapted from the 1872 translation by Mrs. H. P. Paull

Text copyright © 2007 by Purple Bear Books Inc.

Illustrations copyright © 2005 by The Art Agency "PiART"

First published in Taiwan in 2006 by Grimm Press

First English-language edition published in 2007 by Purple Bear Books Inc., New York.

For more information about our books, visit our website: purplebearbooks.com

Library of Congress Cataloging-in-Publication Data is available.

This edition prepared by Cheshire Studio.

TRADE EDITION

ISBN-10: 1-933327-30-8

ISBN-13: 978-1-933327-30-3

1 3 5 7 9 TE 10 8 6 4 2

LIBRARY EDITION

ISBN-10: 1-933327-31-6

ISBN-13: 978-1-933327-31-0

1 3 5 7 9 LE 10 8 6 4 2

Printed in Taiwan

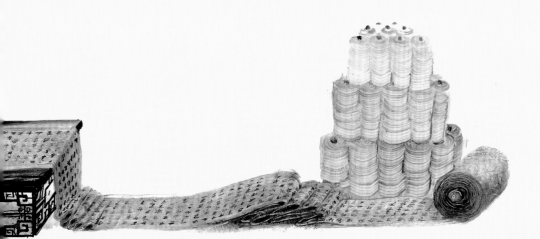